CHÚCARO

·THE·NEWBERY·HONOR·ROLL·

CHÚCARO
WILD PONY OF THE PAMPA

FRANCIS KALNAY

Illustrations by Julian de Miskey

WALKER & COMPANY   NEW YORK

Published in the United States of America in 1993 by Walker Publishing Company,
Inc.

Published simultaneously in Canada by Thomas Allen & Son Canada, Limited,
Markham, Ontario

Library of Congress Cataloging-in-Publication Data
Kalnay, Francis.
    Chúcaro : wild pony of the Pampa / Francis Kalnay ; illustrations
by Julian de Miskey.
        p. cm.
    Summary: Adventures of a boy and his pony on the Argentine Pampa.
    ISBN 0-8027-7387-7 (p)
    [1. Argentina—Fiction. 2. Ponies—Fiction.] I. De Miskey,
Julian, ill. II. Title.
PZ7.K126Ch 1993
[Fic]—dc20   92-18964
                                                                         CIP
                                                                          AC

PRINTED IN THE UNITED STATES OF AMERICA

10

To Pedro Andrés Jorge

CONTENTS

FOREWORD

The vast grass-covered plain that sweeps down from the Andes Mountains to the Atlantic Ocean is called the *Pampa* by the Indians. The name means prairie, but picture the Pampa generously: a rich meadow extending far beyond the horizon, like the sea. The *gauchos*, who are the cowboys of the Pampa, sometimes ride day after day after day across these grasslands and do not come to the end of them.

This is the story of some people who lived in the heart of the Argentine Pampa—men, women, boys—of one boy especially, and a horse, a very special horse.

CHÚCARO

1

LASSO

Some growing corn has golden hair, some yellow, some red, some brown. But look, there is one stalk with locks as black as the night, and if you creep up close, you will find this hair is not growing out of corn. It belongs to Pedro, the twelve-year-old son of the *Vaquero*. He was hunting for the hiding place of the *perdiz*, which is like our partridge—a little more shy perhaps, for even Pedro's sharp eyes couldn't find it. He was near the edge of the cornfield, searching through the jungle of stalks, when he saw something strange, and he stopped, stock-still. Hidden in the tall, leafy corn, Pedro held his breath and stared.

There, ankle-deep in the luscious alfalfa a short distance from where Pedro stood, a wild pony was having his breakfast. Maybe because he was so terribly hungry, or maybe because it was his first taste of this forbidden food, the pony acted as though he had never in his life tasted grass so juicy and sweet. He grazed in keen delight. His mouth watered and foamed and formed bubbles, beautiful green like jade. Each time his mouth was full, he lifted his head and, while chewing, looked about him. The air, heavy with the sweet scent of corn, made his nostrils quiver with delight. Once or twice he stood still, hesitant. Quietly Pedro stepped a little closer and watched the pony's every movement. He expected the horse to leave the alfalfa for the corn, but no, the grass was too delicious.

Pedro had been born in the *estancia*, where horses were kept without number, and he had ridden ponies ever since he was five. But he had never seen anything like this one! Pink certainly is a most unusual color for a horse, and Pedro could hardly believe his eyes. The color of the pink geraniums in the owners' patio, he thought, and no doubt just as soft. He noticed that the pony's ankles were pure white and looked new, like the socks worn by the wealthy village boys on Sundays. The pony also had snow-white beauty spots, one on his left cheek, one on the right. They suited him exactly.

"If only I could lasso him," pondered the boy, but he decided this was far too big a prize to take a chance of losing. So instead, he crept back to the Vaquero's hut and brought his father along.

"*Que maravilla!*" cried the old man. "You were right, son; there isn't another pony like it. But, no, no, I couldn't risk throwing the noose on him."

"You must; you have done it hundreds of times," begged Pedro. "Why couldn't you do it now?"

The old man spread his palms. "My hands are no longer the same, Pedrito," he said with a bitter smile. "When you get old, your hands shake, my boy, and are no longer safe for the lasso."

But there was something else, they both knew, beside advancing age that made the Vaquero's hands unsteady. The boy had noticed for some time that his father no longer sipped the wine with his meals but gulped it down

fast and furiously as if dying of thirst. When his mother died, Pedrito was barely a year old. People at the ranch said that after the burial the Vaquero was no longer himself. He used to be strong as an ox and always full of fun. With his strength went also his pride. He was usually in rags, to which nobody objected, and it was sad that he didn't seem to care.

"Do you want him badly, Pedrito?" asked the old man, bending down.

"I would give anything to have him, Papa," whispered the boy.

"Well, then there is only one man who can get him for you. You just sit quietly here, and I'll go back for Juan."

Not for a second did Pedro let the horse out of his sight. Lying on his stomach to have a clearer view between the rows of corn, and with his mouth wide open, he watched the slightest movement of the pony. It took hardly more than a few minutes for the gaucho to reach the place, but to Pedro it seemed hours.

"Please get him quick," begged Pedro before Juan was even near. "He may run off and I'll never see him any more!"

"Now, wait, wait; don't get so excited!" quieted the gaucho. "Let me look at him first."

"There, there," whispered the boy, his cheeks aflame.

"*Caramba!* What a perfect colt! A pure *criollo*, if I ever saw one! I wonder if it has been branded. Have you noticed any marks on him?"

"I don't see any, but what do we care?"

"We can't lasso him if he belongs to some other rancho, you silly boy."

"But we'll have to lasso him first to see the brand. You can't notice it from here." The boy's voice was hoarse with excitement.

"Now, there is something in that. Wait."

The Pampa is an enormous land, and there are some mighty fine gauchos there. But there never was a man more skillful with the rope than Juan. The usual method with wild ponies was to herd them into the corral. But Juan looked down upon that kind of sport. He preferred to swing the noose, which he always prepared himself, out in the open field. This was ordinarily considered a risky chance, but not with Juan. His eagle eye measured the distance to the inch, his timing was as exact as a fine cuckoo clock.

You could hear a slight whistle as the lasso spun through the air, and seconds later Juan gently pulled in the rope. There stood the little horse right in front of

them, a bunch of alfalfa still hanging from his mouth. His frightened eyes were wide open and wild. As the boy quietly advanced, the horse reared frantically and made a desperate effort to escape. He would have dragged an ordinary man along, but not Juan—no fear! Juan held the end of the rope tight—he was strong and obstinate, like a bull.

His legs spread wide and his eyes filled with tears, the pony was now a pitiful sight. Pedro could no longer stand it. "Let him go; please let him free," he begged.

"What is the matter with you?" Juan stamped his foot, indignant. "A moment ago you begged me to lasso him, and now you want me to let him go. Some gaucho you are! Now run back to the ranch and bring me a piece of rope for a halter, and run quick!"

As soon as Pedro left, the gaucho slackened the rope so that the pony would feel more at ease. Then they looked each other straight in the eye—the pony in horror and the man with a big, melting smile. "Now, now," he said. "Relax. I am not half as tough as I look, and some day, I bet, you and I will be real friends. You'll see."

The colt pricked up his ears. "Easy, easy," said the gaucho, advancing no more than a step, his voice soft and soothing. "Turn your head and look at me sideways; that's right! Now I can see that you are getting reason-

able, except for those shiny eyes. Crying? What a shame!
Here, try this alfalfa. There is nothing like it in the whole
province!" He threw a bunch of fresh grass to the pony.
"Now I know perfectly well that you won't touch it, not
yet. I know how you feel. All I want is to show you the
kind of food we grow here! What do you think? Why are
you looking at my left hand? Would you like to know
what's in it? It is a *rehenque*, my whip. I seldom use it.
I see you don't like it. All right, I'll throw it away. There
it goes, you see? Now what is worrying you? My little
mustache? Sorry, I can't take that off so easily, not even
for you. But you'll get used to it, like everybody else.
May I come a step nearer now? Gently, gently. Don't
shy away. I want to know your name. I am a fool to ask.
You wouldn't know, even if you had one. When I was a
young kid, I had a nice little pony, quite wild like you,
and everybody called him Chúcaro. Chúcaro is just the
right name for a good horse like you. You, too, seem to
like it. You even seem to like me! If that's so, I'll pick
you some corn. You don't have to eat it, just smell it.
So."

When Pedro returned with the rope for the halter, he
simply couldn't believe his eyes.

"The pony doesn't seem to be afraid of you, Juan. What
did you do to him?"

"Nothing. We only had a little chat."

"You really think he understood what you said?"

"Every word of it, and perhaps even more."

"You don't say!"

"Well, you'll see."

"Did you find any brand on him?"

"Not a trace. Except those white spots on his cheeks, but he was born with them. Don't touch him yet, Pedro; just talk to him."

"I wonder what his name is?"

"Chúcaro."

"Chúcaro? How do you know that is his name?"

"Because it fits him perfectly," smiled the gaucho. "A name is like a *sombrero*. It must fit the owner."

2

OMBÙ

When you are walking in a forest, you seldom notice a
single tree. How different it is when you are riding over
the flat, boundless Pampa, where for miles and miles you
see nothing but grass. Then all of a sudden you sight a
tree and exclaim, "Look there! A tree!" Yes, a real tree,
and your heart goes out to it.

It is an *ombù*, the lonely tree of the Pampa. The trunk
is fat, the branches widespread, with large, waxy leaves.
And it has a big, soft heart. It will offer what you want
most—shade!

Not far from the tree you will probably find a hut or a

tiny house. The hut may be made of mud, mixed with cornstalks, or—don't be shocked—of horse-dung and mud.

You will see more and more of such huts as you look around—some close together, some far apart. Gauchos, shepherds, pigherds, *medianeros*, who farm on shares, live in them. Then if your eyes are very sharp or you have field glasses ready, you may see a green spot in the distance. It is a park around a beautiful mansion. This is where the *patrón*, the owner, lives. You will also see wide fields of wheat, oats, and corn, and vast grazing land for the cattle.

Now, all this that you have just seen, and miles beyond, belongs to the patrón. It is his estancia.

You may lie down under that ombú tree. Its shade is so inviting. But if you are not on speaking terms with ants and crickets and other little creatures playing hide-and-seek in the grass, you may prefer to sit in a chair. If you are lucky, you may find a gaucho's chair. It is made of the hipbones of cows, firmly tied together, and the seat is rawhide. You'll find it very comfortable—but beware! When the sun goes down, you'd better get up and move your chair away from the tree. It is bedtime for the chickens, and before long you will find them roosting all over the tree!

3

THE CASITA

Between that old ombù tree and the tallest windmill of the ranch, there stood a little hut, which belonged to Juan. From the outside, this modest little *casita*, with its adobe walls and corrugated tin roof, did not seem to differ from the rest of the huts that were dotted like matchboxes around the ranch. But the moment you were

13

inside the house, which had only one room, you would be sure that it belonged to Juan. The door hung from a single hinge so that it was conveniently half-closed, half-open. On the wall opposite the door, there was a small opening the size of two bricks. If it had been covered by glass, it might have been called a window. Juan referred to it as a "hole." Really it would have been difficult to get along without that hole. Whenever Juan needed something from the house, he would usually reach for it through the hole instead of bending down to go through the doorway, which was four inches lower than he. Or if Pedro was around, he would say to the boy, "Get me that piece of wire from the house. You'll find it right near the hole." True enough, Pedro always found it, for everything that did not belong in the chest could always be found "around the hole."

There is nothing easier in the world than to drive a good-sized nail into a wall built of mud. That may be one reason why Juan had so many pictures hung on his walls.

Now, take that photograph on the right side of the window. An awful "mug" with a long dark beard, and under it printed, MURDERER WANTED—1000 PESOS RE-WARD. Why did he nail that on the wall? It was given to him some ten years before by the village policeman, who regarded him as the most capable gaucho on either side

14

of the Salados River. "Hold onto this picture, Juan," he had said. "Maybe some day this fellow will come around the ranch, and if any gaucho can capture him, you're the one to do it!" No use denying that Juan was flattered by these words, but since he had a little practical sense, he risked the question: "And what are my chances of capturing him?"

"Ten times better than winning the big prize in the lottery," said the policeman with emphasis.

"And what does that mean?" asked Juan.

"Well, as a police official I don't like to commit myself. I'd rather ask you this question: Did you ever win the big prize in the lottery?"

"No, never."

"All right. Multiply that by ten. The results are your chances. But you can easily figure this out for yourself."

He had never bothered to figure it out. Instead he nailed the picture on the wall, just in case . . .

MURDERER
WANTED
1000 PESOS
REWARD

There are few rivers or streams on the Pampa proper, and those flow quietly as if asleep. Maybe this explains why Juan had picked a picture of the most spectacular body of water to decorate the left-hand side of the window: "The Waterfalls of the Iguazú."

Juan never bothered to read the papers. He considered that a pastime for city folks who had nothing better to do. There was, however, one paper, *La Prensa* of Buenos Aires, for which he had a great respect, although he had never read a single copy of it. It was in *La Prensa* that the beautiful full-page photograph of the waterfalls of the Iguazú had appeared. He was always grateful to the *estanciero's* servant who gave it to him.

For several days after the picture was hung, Juan did not send Pedro when he wanted something "around the hole." Instead, he himself went for it straight through the doorway. And he always lingered just to admire the picture of the marvelous falls. There was a little map boxed into one corner of it that showed the location of the falls between Argentina and Brazil. Sometimes Juan would take a nail and scratch lines on the wall, indicating the road he would follow someday to view this most wonderful spectacle in the world, which no one whom he had ever met had actually seen. . . . There is also Paraguay, he thought, so close, where the finest *maté*

grows, that sweet and bitter tea the gaucho sucks through a silver tube from a hollow gourd—maybe five, maybe ten times a day!

More pictures hung above the rusty, old iron bed, which, by the way, was just the bare frame with not a stitch of bedding on it. It was pushed against the wall, and right in the center above it hung "The Good Shepherd"—Christ guiding a flock of golden sheep. The whole flock of sheep was painted gold. It was a beautiful picture, entirely worthy of the fancy leather frame around it. Juan

17

had spent a whole week making it. The picture itself was the gift of a traveling missionary who was grateful to Juan for having shown him a short cut to the train.

Then there were above the door picture post cards from the biggest towns—Buenos Aires, Rosario, La Plata—but only one actually addressed to him. This was from a girl he had met many, many years before at a carnival. Oh, how eager he was to answer that card, how often he had sat down and begun to write! But what's the use of spoiling a pen, breaking your back—and your heart—for a girl who forgot to give her address!

There was no table in the room, nor any chairs. But there was something else, which was even more useful— a chest. In a pinch, you could use the top as a card table or to write on, but Juan never did either. He kept his personal things in the chest. Anyone allowed to lift the top would see a brown *poncho* with fine white stripes. Ponchos like that can't be found so easily nowadays. It was of llama wool, so firmly woven that neither heat, nor rain, nor cold could get through it. An Indian from the Andes had given it to him for one silver coin and a pair of boots. This poncho was reserved for Sundays, as was the black sombrero that lay next to it. In the folds of the poncho, he kept his guitar. Wrapped in an old *corralera*, a collarless gaucho blouse, were a pair of leather stirrups,

18

heavily carved in a chain design. They had belonged to Juan's father, a half-breed Indian gaucho. After his father's death, his mother had sent him a package with these keepsakes. Besides the stirrups and the corralera, which had been his father's wedding shirt, there were two kerchiefs, a fancy silver tube for sipping maté, and a wide leather belt for gala occasions. The belt was very heavy, as it was studded with silver coins and buttons, and it had extra leather pockets for money, and straps for knife and quirt. It must have been very, very old, because the silver studs were almost black. It had a peculiar odor that reminded you, all at the same time, of a perspiring horse, fresh cabbage, and onion soup with Parmesan cheese. This strong, exotic perfume permeated every single article Juan wore, including his shirts, kerchiefs, and even his *vincha*, his special headdress. Now don't make any mistake. Juan was usually clean and neat. This particular odor really belonged to him. It was a family aroma, handed down from father to son through this remarkable belt. Both men and beasts became used to it and rather liked it. Pedro found it especially convenient, particularly on Sunday evenings when more than the usual group were seated arund the campfire. By means of it he could single out Juan in the dark from quite a distance.

The two kerchiefs are worthy of special mention. After

19

all, a gaucho is not a gaucho without his kerchief! He may give you his boots, his nice baggy trousers, or even his last shirt, but he won't part with his kerchief. Without his kerchief around his neck, he would feel shy as if he were naked. Now, Juan had a yellow kerchief for every-day use, while the two in his chest were red and blue. If Sunday happened to be nice and bright, he wore the red, but when it rained, or the cold *pampero* blew from the southwest, he tied the blue kerchief around his neck. His friend Pedro could tell the weather just by looking at him.

It's too bad he only had one red kerchief, for it really was very becoming to him. It gave an additional strength and light to his dark complexion, his long eagle nose, and to those deep-set brown eyes, which were, at the same time, sharp, intelligent, and kind. One thing he missed pitifully—a beard. The little black mustache, which curved and pointed toward his nostrils, seemed so insignificant and lonely. Only when he smiled, the little mustache began to feel fine, junping up and down on his wide, red lips. So whenever you saw the little mustache jump, you could rest assured that all of them were in high mood—Juan, the mustache, and Pedro.

Pedro really belonged to Juan. He was as much a part of him as his kerchief. From early morning till nightfall,

the boy was always at Juan's heels. It was really Juan and not the Vaquero who raised the child. He took charge of him soon after Pedro's mother died. There was an unwritten agreement between the two men, and both knew that, for all concerned, it was for the best.

Juan didn't spoil the boy; nobody could accuse him of

that. There were two things he knew to perfection—the training of horses and young cowboys.

It's true that every Sunday morning he would enter his house, reach down into the chest, open the little pocket in the old belt, and give Pedro a few pennies for that long stick of hard candy with pink and green stripes in it. But that certainly couldn't spoil a tough boy like Pedro!

The big chest and the lovely things in it, the old iron bed, and the beautiful pictures on the wall were the real treasures of Juan's casita, his little house. But the truth will surprise you—he never spent a night in his house!

His sleeping place was far out in the field. It consisted of a cart with two high wheels. The top and the sides of the cart were covered with leather. It was a convenient bedroom, easy to move. Sometimes the cart stood near the ombù tree; at other times it stood nearer to the cattle. Inside it was cosy, although there was no furniture or any sort of decoration. A thick, heavy mattress, filled with straw, covered the entire floor. It was very easy to keep in order. Once every year, shortly after the harvest, he would fill the mattress with fresh straw. And once or twice a year he would go to the big barrel standing at the end of the trough under the windmill and wash his blanket in cold water and spread it out on the grass. The sun did the rest. The sides of the cart in warm weather were always kept open, both for fresh air and because when Juan went to bed, he liked to sit up for a while and watch. He liked to watch the distant lights, and listen to a strange music—the Pampa sounds. And so many things to think about—but the moment he lay down, he fell asleep almost before he could finish his yawn.

Sometimes he dreamt about that picture card he had received and about the answer he had never written.

4

CURRYCOMB

Juan led the pony, and Pedro walked at a safe distance behind. But when they reached Juan's house, the boy ran ahead.

"I think we ought to put Chúcaro in your casita for the night. Let's remove the door; it's only hanging by a thread anyway."

Juan was struck dumb. His right hand resting on his

hip, he just stood silent for a while, his eyes measuring the house, the horse, and the boy.

"This is going a little bit too far, Pedro," he said at last with a smile. "If it were up to you, you would put the horse in the bed, give him a nightshirt and *La Prensa* to read."

"But I thought your house would be the safest place. Besides, you never sleep in the casita anyway."

"Well, if I can't sleep shut up in the casita, how could Chúcaro stand it? I know his feelings as well as mine."

"Just for a single night? I would feel better knowing he is safe."

"Safe? Why, if four walls make me jumpy, they would make him crazy with pain. He is a criollo pony. The finest, don't forget! You shouldn't hurt his feelings like that. . . . No, Pedrito, that wouldn't do! We'll fence him off in the corral for a few days. As long as he can feel the Pampa grass under his hoofs, some oats in his mouth, and see the sky above his head, he won't feel the place is a prison. But first bring me the currycomb. You'll find it around the hole."

When Chúcaro first caught sight of the currycomb, he was so frightened that you could see the whites of his eyes. And at the first touch of the brush, he jumped and trembled as if he were shell-shocked.

"If he acts like that, we'd better tie him to the kicking strap," said Juan for the benefit of both Chúcaro and Pedro.

But the kicking strap was really not needed. When the pony felt the gentle strokes of the brush, he relaxed and you could tell he was thrilled. No doubt it reminded him of certain fence posts and tree trunks he used to rub his neck against. But this seemed a hundred times more satisfying.

Now scratching, you will agree, is a very personal thing. Few of us practice it in company, and when we do, it is completely absent-minded. With animals, scratching is a serious business. It is as much a part of their toilet as washing our faces in the morning is for us. Our animal friends don't mind scratching even in high society. Observe that they practice two kinds of scratching. One is a quick act, as, for instance, the dog when trying to brush off an arrogant flea. This sort of thing is ordinary routine. The other type of scratching occurs only at certain times of the day or the night and is performed in leisure, ceremoniously. With some, it may take only half an hour, while with others it may last— like a double-feature program—half the afternoon. Some animals on this occasion will lie down and relax and have their colleagues do the work for them. Others prefer not

27

to share the pleasure and do it all by themselves. Some do it with their claws, some with their tongue, their nose and teeth, or feet, and some, like the armadillo, prefer the tail to do the whole business from A to Z.

Horses have a different technique, limited to one of these—rub against a tree trunk or telephone pole, or roll over on the grass. Whatever the method, it is a lot of fun. But, frankly, neither is entirely satisfactory. There are a few sheltered parts of a pony, like the tiny spot under his elbow, which he can never get at by rubbing against any kind of pole or rolling back and forth till doomsday.

Now you can understand how Chúcaro reacted to the sweet tickle of the currycomb. Never had he experienced such delights except when his mother used to rub her nose against his neck. Stroke after stroke, inch by inch, all over his body he felt the same amusing sensation. He knew that it wasn't the brush only but those kindly fingers that offered him joy and begged for friendship.

5

TEARS

Chúcaro was kept in the corral for about a week. Each morning, after the roundup of the cattle, Juan would visit him. But he couldn't get there early enough to be ahead of his friend Pedrito. Each would bring to the pony some delicacy, a piece of carrot, a handful of oats, or a little piece of sugar. And they would take turns in brushing his lovely coat, which really was like those geranium flowers—a shade between yellow, brown, and pink—growing in the patio of the estanciero. Sometimes Juan would tie the pony to a rope and let Pedro give him some exercise running around in circles.

The news traveled fast around the estancia; it passed from mouth to mouth. "Pedro has a new pony! You never saw anything like it! He has a pinkish coat like the geranium petals in the *patio* of Señor Muñez. He has four little white socks, like those you see on city children on Sundays. He is supposed to be a wild colt, and yet he eats out of your hand! You can't help petting him. Just go and see!"

And they all came, one after another—Carlos and José, gaucho friends; Mr. and Mrs. Pizetti, the medianeros who cultivated a stretch of the cornfield; all the "swallows" or harvest workers; the shepherds and pigherds; the overseers; the Italian, Hungarian, Polish, and Slovak immigrants and their children, who rented a piece of the land or worked for "half-and-half"; the blacksmith, the bookkeeper, the tractor-driver, the chauffeur, and even the veterinary came. On the Pampa, like any other place, some faces seem hard, others soft; some cold and others warm. There wasn't a face, though, that failed to light up when Chúcaro approached. Some stroked Chúcaro's neck or kissed his cheek. Others just shook their heads enviously and said, "Why couldn't I have such luck?"

There was an Indian gaucho who offered Pedro two beautiful ponies broken in for riding, with saddle, stirrups, and all the proper fittings, if only he would give

him Chúcaro. A young Italian farmer offered a pair of
slightly worn black boots—just a little too big—twenty-
five sacks of corn and a rehenque with a silver handle.
And the assistant bookkeeper was ready to give him all

32

his accumulated wealth, which he said amounted to thirty pesos and some change, plus a harmonica, highly polished and beautiful, which, however, didn't work.

Your guess is correct. Pedro politely refused every one of the offers. However, at the bookkeeper's bid, he became so excited one could almost see the blood rush to his cheeks.

"I know that thirty pesos is a lot of silver," he said, "but I wouldn't give up Chúcaro if you gave me a million and a million and, on the top of that, the whole world." So everybody saw there was no room to bargain.

Pedro got up earlier than usual one morning—long before Juan was up. In fact, he made quite certain that Juan was asleep. Then without the customary blindfolding or the use of the kicking strap, he jumped on Chúcaro's back.

The first few days after that, to tell you the truth, were very trying to both of them.

Juan had expected that the pony would be ready for his first tryout with saddle about three weeks after his capture. So when he thought the time had come, and he and Pedro met in the corral, Juan threw sheepskin and a rough saddle on the pony. He was amazed that Chúcaro stood perfectly quiet.

"How strange," remarked the gaucho. "Chúcaro

doesn't seem to mind it! I've never seen a wild colt carry the saddle without blindfolding. *Que milagro!*" he cried. "No jumping, no kicking, no biting! Well, my friend, you might as well jump on him."

"You try him first," said Pedro with downcast eyes.

"What's the matter, Pedrito? Are you afraid?"

"No, Señor," and Pedro's eyes were still fixed on his own bare feet.

"I don't understand. There's something funny about this. I never heard of your refusing a first ride!"

The boy stepped back and sat down on the ground. It took some effort to answer, "I want you to have the pleasure now."

Juan stared at the horse, then at Pedro. Then he understood.

"You shouldn't have done it, you rascal! I told you to go easy with the horse. You don't appreciate a good pony when you have one. He should be treated gently, as you treat a friend." He threw his sombrero over the corral fence. He was angry.

"I'm sorry, Juan," said the boy, and his voice quavered. "Chúcaro didn't seem to mind it. It was so tempting . . ."

"Tempting, eh? Well, I give up! I can't be bothered with two pets at one time. Get out of my sight!! I'm through!"

Pedro got up. He felt his throat dry and swollen, and he could hardly drag his bare feet through the dust. He stumbled along and was just able to reach the corral gate when he burst into tears. He had to sit down, for his heart seemed too heavy and his legs too weak to go further. He turned toward the gatepost and buried his head in his hands. Now he was sobbing, but no sound was heard. As his fingers pressed his eyes, everything became terribly dark. It seemed as if a black, black cloud covered the whole world, and he, Pedro, all alone with no place to go, must face the oncoming storm.

Juan fussed with the straps, patted Chúcaro's neck, unlatched the stirrups, and fumbled with the saddle again. You could see that he was just killing time, absent-minded and miserable. "Why did I tell the boy to get out? And suppose someday he should really clear out—out of my life," he tortured himself. After all, no harm had been done. He stole a look at Pedro. "Why doesn't he cry out loud, at least?" He could see only the boy's high forehead and flat, funny nose. His hands ached to stroke that dark head, to lift him in his arms. He longed to say, "Don't cry, Pedrito. No harm has been done. Just jump on Chúcaro and everything will be all right. We are old friends; you ought to know that." But he was too clumsy to put all that into words, so instead he threw his yellow kerchief at Pedro's feet and said, "You'd better wipe your face with that and bring my red kerchief from the chest, you—touchy little lamb!"

The storm was over.

As if shot from a gun, the boy ran to the casita and in a jiffy ran back waving the kerchief in his hand.

For the first time in many years Juan lifted Pedro up into the saddle.

With his right hand holding the bridle rein, and with his left furtively wiping away a few stray tears, Pedrito sat up straight in the saddle, secure and proud. Suddenly he turned to the gaucho. "Why did you ask for your red kerchief? It isn't Sunday."

"Well . . . I don't know. . . . After all . . . when you think of it . . . Chúcaro and you riding out for the first time . . . and everything. Who says it isn't like Sunday?" and he quickly turned back to open the gate. He leaned against the gatepost and watched Chúcaro gallop by. Two graceful heads held high, Pedro and Chúcaro heading for the open fields—they seemed one. Thrilled by the sight and absorbed in his thoughts, Juan stood at the corral gate for a long, long time.

All of a sudden he sniffed and smelled acacia wood burning. Again he sniffed and smelled roast beef, and realized that he was getting hungry.

6

GITANA, THE GYPSY

It would be quite unfair to neglect Juan's horse, Gitana. The name really describes her—a gypsy girl. If you will agree that gypsy girls are dark, temperamental, and graceful, fond of fancy ribbons, huge silver buttons, and such, and full of fun and wanderlust, then Gitana was truly a *gitana*. People who know gypsies best claim they are cunning. If this is true, then Juan's horse was a gypsy thoroughbred!

She was about nine, just nicely plump, and wore an elegant light-brown fur coat. She was sure-footed and fast. Gitana seemed proud of her fancy bridle and bit which were pure silver. Her capacity for feed was tremendous, and the only thing that was even bigger was her insatiable wanderlust. If Juan left her at the south end of the field, a few minutes later she would be grazing nonchalantly way up in the north. More than once when Juan needed her urgently, he had to look for Gitana in the village, fifteen solid miles away.

And what is your guess, did Gitana welcome Chúcaro?

People who travel a lot for fun, like wanderers, globe-trotters, beachcombers, hoboes, and tramps, are seldom jealous. So you see, Gitana and Chúcaro almost immediately became friends. Although the difference in age was great, they had several essentials in common. Both loved adventure. They seemed to understand each other in their own horse-language. Both liked to use their heads. Yes, they were intelligent. And also they were good-hearted and loyal to their masters.

The very moment Gitana saw Chúcaro, she felt friendly toward that beautiful colt. However, soon she found out that Chúcaro was young and inexperienced. He would need a lot of help from her. Gitana, as you know, had a lot of horse sense, was clever in all directions, and she was a great comfort to Chúcaro.

7

MEAT, MATÉ, MUSIC

There is no meal simpler to prepare than a gaucho dinner. Provided you have a little fire built out in the open
field, then you need only two things—a big chunk of
meat and a solid iron spike. That's all.

The gaucho seldom eats vegetables. He does not cultivate them and, though they may be pretty to look at,
vegetables to him are—chicken feed!

Occasionally, when the fancy takes him, he may prepare a potful of *puchero*. This puchero is second cousin to an Irish stew, or a Hungarian *gulyás*.

Like any good stew the puchero is full of surprises. If you just dig in, a spoonful at a time, the thrill will remind you of a package party. You don't know what's coming next. Here a chunk of spicy sausage, there a slice of cabbage, then a piece of ham, next a carrot or a potato big as your fist.

Don't ever be afraid, when you are invited to partake of puchero, that you may not like it. You are bound to like *some* part of it. But if you flatly refuse to try it at all, then the fault is yours. There could be nothing wrong with the puchero prepared fresh on the Pampa.

Your true gaucho is a meat-eater, if there ever was one. Meat! That's his *business*. He rides it, he herds it, and he eats it.

The gaucho needs no kitchen, no utensils, and no fancy service. Just let him pierce a big chunk of meat, say twenty pounds of beef, with an iron spit. He sticks this into the ground at an angle above the fire. The rest is easy. He pokes the fire, turns the meat around, and pokes it with his knife, which is always sharp, as are his teeth.

If a juicy medium-done beefsteak is to your liking, sit

down near the fire and help yourself. The gaucho loves company. And he loves to talk and to listen to stories, especially after the choicest cuts of the roast are gone. He hasn't eaten too much, possibly only a couple of pounds, and if you too say "*basta*—enough" he will throw the rest to the dogs. Now is the time to place the kettle

on the fire to have hot water ready for the *yerba maté*. He has his hollow gourd at hand and the ornamental silver tube with which he sips the bitter drink. You will find him somewhat impatient for his maté. When at last he has the taste of that famous Paraguayan beverage in his mouth, he settles back contented. If it's chilly, you will see him crouched near the fire, his poncho pulled close, happy just to watch the flames. And after a sip or two from the gourd, he'll turn to you and say, "Well, *amigo mío*, unless you have some interesting story to tell, I'll sing you a lovely song that Carmela taught me the other night. Let me just reach for my guitar. . . ." Any gaucho may tell you that.

But not Juan.

To begin with, Juan seldom went to village dances and parties where one has a chance to meet new girls and new songs. He preferred to stay around the camp, dance with the same girls, or sit in front of his fire late into the night and sing the old-time gaucho songs. He had a lovely ringing voice, and sometimes, from a distance, it sounded as mellow as the chimes of the chapel at the estancia. Although somewhat shy, he didn't mind singing in company when the gauchos around were his friends, but he was at his best when Pedrito was his only audience. Then he would lie on his back on the grass, facing

44

the sky, and sing song after song as if he had one apiece for each little star. And once in a while he would sit up, and for no apparent reason both he and Pedro would laugh out loud.

"That was a jolly old song, Pedrito. What do you say?"

The ponies, too, enjoyed the music. You would often find them grazing near the fire, and though you may not believe it, they really were listening.

Many evenings, when stories had their turn, Chúcaro hardly stirred a step from his favorite spot near the fire. When Pedrito felt tired, he would climb on his pony's back, fold his arms around Chúcaro's neck, and cling there, listening to the story until his eyes closed. It might

be that an outburst of laughter would wake him up, and drowsy as he was, he would try to catch the drift of the story.

Then once more his hands would steal around the neck of Chúcaro, and he would whisper in the pony's ear. "You tell me the rest of the story tomorrow. Good night, my Chúcaro."

Then Juan would lift the boy from the pony, quietly lay him down on the broad seat of the cart, and cover him with a poncho.

8

WHAT THE MAYORDOMO DIDN'T KNOW WAS NOT WORTH KNOWING

The *mayordomo* was a big man on every count. Number one, he was well over six feet tall; two, he was in charge of the whole estancia; number three, he knew everything about everything; and four, everyone stood in awe of him.

Everyone, that is, except Juan.

Now if you think that directing a big estancia is child's play, you are mistaken. A good-sized Argentine estancia is not like a farm. It is much larger than that. It is as big as fifty or a hundred farms joined together. In the midst of it there is a separate small farm, where everything is specially cultivated, and there are lovely gardens surrounding a beautiful, great big house. This is where the owner, the estanciero, lives with his family, whenever he is there.

Let's suppose that you are an estanciero, who, by the way, is also called the patrón. The first and most important thing for you to do is to find a good mayordomo, for a mayordomo is the one who is put in charge of the whole estancia, who knows everything about everything and is obeyed by all. When you've found the right one, then if you wish, you can say "*Adiós*" to all your worries and go merrily on your way.

It's hard to say offhand where you may go. You may go to Buenos Aires, the largest city in all South America, where you will probably stay until the hot summer arrives in December. There are many, many things to do in Buenos Aires. You may keep a stable there and watch your own horses at the races. You may be a polo fan, or you may be interested in exhibiting your prize bulls at the cattle show. It is even possible that you may spend

48

most of your time visiting museums and theaters or studying at the university. Some estancieros spend all their time in offices, up to their necks in business of every sort. Others just stretch out in hammocks in their patios and listen to tango music all day long. Still others prefer to do nothing—and do it well!

But out in the country, life is entirely different.

The mayordomo's face is bronzed and ruddy. He is always running back and forth and is always excited, because hardly anything is exactly to his liking. Early in the day you may see him in his office, giving orders to his small army of overseers and foremen. Then off he dashes. Half an hour later, you'll find him with the vet-

erinary, watching the cattle as they are forced through a chute full of creosote to prevent sickness.

You may stay for a long time watching the poor animals being driven through this unexpected bath, which you can be sure, from their actions, they detest. However, the mayordomo has no time to waste. He is now far out in the wheat fields, arguing with an Italian medianero. The medianero and his family are entrusted with a good-sized field to cultivate. The seed and farming machines are furnished by the estanciero, but the medianero does all the work from planting to harvesting. After the harvest, half of the crop goes to the patrón and half belongs to the medianero. There is always a little room for argument.

"You agreed to give me that, and I agreed to give you this. But since you haven't given me that, I am not going to give you this." And so it goes. But in the end everything quiets down. The mayordomo is a powerful man.

Next you see him galloping madly off toward a little gaucho hut. He keeps track of everything on a sheet of paper full of figures. How many head of cattle have been herded ready to be shipped to market?

"Tomorrow," he tells the gaucho foreman, "twenty additional bulls are to be driven in from the north grazing fields. They have to be thrown and ringed."

Now he is once more on his way back to the office. A telegram must be sent. The big tractor has broken down. The harvest is almost here. "Rush parts immediately. We must have them without fail!"

A whole crowd of people are waiting for him at the office. One complains that the sheep have got into the garden. How did they get there? They broke through the fence. Whose flock was it? God only knows. What shall we do? . . . An Indian stands there fumbling with his greasy hat. The baby died last night. No! Good God! What a pity! She had such a sweet little face and seemed so well and strong. "Yes, yes—you can put your mind at rest. We'll take care of everything. . . . Here's a telegram from the patrón. They are coming—that reminds me! What is the lazy plumber doing all day long? Isn't that bathroom ready yet? . . . Look at this! Why—Giovanni, what beautiful roses! Imagine growing those on the Pampa. Where did you plant them? On that little patch behind the stable—well, well! . . ."

And that's how it went all day long. But he was able to handle it all, for the mayordomo was a smart man and had to know everything about everything.

But he didn't know anything about Chúcaro.

That's what you think!

9

THE RED KERCHIEF—A MYSTERY

Don't let people deceive you with the idea that some mysteries remain uncovered. There is only one mystery: that sooner or later every mystery is solved.

Take the case of Juan's red kerchief. You will remember that Juan threw his yellow kerchief to Pedrito to wipe his face, which was all streaked with dust and tears, and that he sent Pedrito for his red kerchief. You will also recall Pedro's surprise at his wearing the red one on any day but Sunday. Then Juan in his own awkward way explained to Pedrito that because he felt happy it seemed to him like Sunday.

Now *quebracho* is the hardest wood that grows in Argentina. It is nearly as hard as stone. If you throw it into water, it sinks. The reason why we talk about it is because there are men who have heads and hearts just as hard as the quebracho. And you can't bend them. Juan was made of an altogether different kind of stuff. He was a gaucho. If he felt like wearing the red kerchief, he wore it, even at the price of breaking his own habit. That's the kind of man he was.

But see what happened!

Again, just for a second, try to remember that particular afternoon when Juan was leaning against the gatepost of the corral. He sniffed and smelled beef roasting somewhere. A few minutes before this, his friend José had dashed past him and noticed that he wore his red kerchief.

And this started the ball rolling.

No sooner had José opened the door of his little hut than he called to his wife Maria, "Something must have happened to Juan."

"Why, what's wrong?"

"I saw him a few minutes ago, and he was wearing his red Sunday kerchief."

"You don't say," she said in astonishment. "Why didn't you ask him what happened?"

"You ought to know him by this time. He is always closemouthed about his private affairs."

"Oh, you men! You are so stupid about things like this. Just a glance at him and I would have known what was on his mind. As a matter of fact, I can guess what has happened."

But at this point, she refused to say more.

Their dinner over, Maria didn't even take time to wash the few dishes. She wrapped her shawl around her and ran as fast as her feet would carry her to her neighbor, Señora Luisa.

"Have you finished the embroidery on that *mantilla* you promised me for Christmas?" Maria began.

"Christmas, did you say?" The old lady was gasping for air. "What on earth is the matter with you, Maria? This is only February, unless they sold me the wrong calendar!"

"Well, can't you give a Christmas present ahead of time if it's badly needed?"

"But *why* do you need it?"

"Don't you know? There's a big wedding coming. Juan is going to get married!"

"*Madonna mia!*" Señora Luisa clasped her hands, in real Italian fashion.

"Well, I must run along. I left the dirty dishes." And off Maria went.

Maria was quite a distance away before Señora Luisa came to her senses. Then she shouted, "Wait a minute, Maria."

"I can't," answered Maria.

"Well, tell me at least who is she, and how do you know?"

"It's that foolish little picture on his wall."

"What picture?" But there was no answer. Maria didn't hear her.

"*Which* picture?" Luisa repeated the question to herself. She was baffled.

Señora Luisa went back to her house and picked up her embroidery. She took a few stitches and then stopped. No, no you can't keep your mind on work when big news like that is going round and round in your head.

She took off her white apron and fixed her hair before the mirror. Fifteen minutes later, her best friend and neighbor, Señora Fulana, the wife of the blacksmith, heard someone knocking at the door. She was startled.

"Who is it?"

"It's me, Luisa. Are you in bed already?"

"My husband is. You can hear him snoring like a steamboat," and Señora Fulana opened the door. "As for myself, my dear Luisa, how could I be in bed when I am right here opening the door? I had an uncle who used to answer like that. Always joking. But how are you, my dear? You seem worried. Is anything wrong?"

"Are you sure that your husband is asleep?"

"He's dead to the world. You can talk freely."

"I can't stay more than a minute, but I know you. You are just like me; you love to get the news while it's hot off the *parrilla*."

"By all means!"

"Well, to make a long story short—Juan is going to get married."

"You don't say! . . . And who is the girl?"

Luisa hesitated. She remembered Maria's saying something about a foolish little picture on his wall. "Tell me, my dear, have you ever been in Juan's hut?"

"Why yes, several times."

"Then you probably have noticed a foolish little picture on his wall. I haven't seen it myself. How does she look?"

"*She?*" cried Señora Fulana. "There must be some mistake. The only foolish picture I remember is of a bearded man, and underneath it says 'murderer wanted—1000 pesos reward.' "

"Oh!" A new thought flashed through Luisa's mind. "Now everything is perfectly clear. There isn't a word of truth in the whole story about the marriage."

"What then?" inquired Señora Fulana.

"Don't you see? All this talk about the marriage is just to cover up the truth."

"And what *is* the truth?"

"The truth is that Juan has captured the murderer!"

"And I bet he has received the one thousand pesos' reward."

"Right you are! With all that money in his pocket, he has, of course, decided to quit his job. He is going straight to Buenos Aires and will live like a *gran señor*."

"And the reason he lassoed Chúcaro is because he wants to enter the pony in the races, I don't doubt."

"Absolutely right."

"Yes, but he would never leave Pedrito behind."

"Of course not. Pedrito will be the jockey. And a mighty good one at that!"

"You bet!"

"Now, let me offer you some maté," said Señora Fulana.

"No, thank you. It is getting late. I must run."

Luisa had already crossed the threshold when she turned back to warn her friend.

"Now, *please* don't breathe a word of this to anyone. We must keep it strictly between ourselves. You know how some folks like to twist things around. And if there is one thing I detest from the bottom of my heart, it is gossip!"

"So do I."

10

SOMETHING IS BREWING AGAIN

Looking at it from an airplane flying high, the Pampa seems vast, bare, and bleak. But the gaucho does not fly so high. With his saddle only three feet from the ground, he sees an entirely different picture. From the airplane the prairie appears dead. But from the saddle you can almost hear the Pampa breathing. Plants, animals, and men, in bright colors and distinct forms, come to the foreground. They may seem asleep, but watch and you'll see—they grow and move and smell and sing. Watching

and kicked, but at last they had to give in. The gauchos' skill and ropes finally did the trick. One after another the bulls tumbled.

This work was hardly finished when word came from the mayordomo that two hundred more cattle must be rounded up, ready for shipment.

"Caramba! Two hundred cattle," Juan protested. "That's a day's work in itself."

"*Mañana*," cried Carlos. "Tomorrow is another day!"

It was past noon when they rode toward the rancho at last. "Let's go over to the Pizettis'," suggested Carlos, "since we are so near. I am dying for some maté. I'm ready to drop!"

There is nothing more reviving to a gancho than a sip of maté when he is tired. So Juan did not even answer. He merely nodded.

The small farm that the Pizettis rented from the patrón was unlike the rest.

"God only knows how they do it," their neighbors would say. "They use the same seed, the same machines and everything. But they always harvest twice as much as we do. They have fruit trees, vegetables, chickens, geese, and even a flower garden and fancy shade trees, I wish somebody could tell me where they get the time and energy."

64

How they did it and when they did it was hard to say. But everybody had to admit that the Pizettis had made a small paradise for themselves.

"It looks as if it were made of sugar!" Pedrito pointed to the little house, neatly painted white and green. "And everything about it smells so sweet and clean."

"Yes, yes," said Juan. "They are the nicest people you ever met."

"What I like most about them," added Carlos, "is that they always tell the truth, even if it hurts. But let's not talk so loud; I see someone dozing on the bench."

"*Hola*, Señora," the gauchos called out to Mrs. Pizetti, who was out in the garden pulling up onions. "Always working, eh?"

"Just a bit of exercise. There is nothing better to take off a little extra flesh. But can I believe my eyes! All our good friends—Carlos, Juan, Pedrito. Well, well, come in to the patio; it's nice and cool there. Make yourselves comfortable, and I'll bring you some maté in a minute."

"But wait," said Carlos. "We don't want to intrude. You seem to have a guest. I saw somebody dozing on the bench with his head under a newspaper."

"Oh," laughed Mrs. Pizetti, "the flies were bothering him. But you'll find he's no stranger. It's the Vaquero."

At the sound of his name, the Vaquero sat up.

"I'm glad that you are here," the old man muttered, still clutching his wine bottle. "I met the mayordomo last evening. . . ."

"Well, what of it?" Carlos and Juan asked at the same time.

"He didn't kill me or anything like that. But why don't you sit down? Come here to the bench, Pedrito."

When all of them were seated around the table, Señora Pizetti brought in a gourd filled with maté. "Pass it around, Juan," she said hospitably. "There is a whole kettle of water on the stove, boiling hot. Just let me know when you need it."

"You had better have a sip first," said Juan to the Vaquero. "Otherwise you'll fall asleep again, and I shall never know what the mayordomo told you."

"Well, I was just leaving the stable when he stopped me. He says, 'I sort of like that new pony you have,' he says. 'He seems gentle, and fast as the devil,' he says."

"You bet!" Juan agreed. "There isn't a pony anywhere to match Chúcaro!"

"And he's smart, too," added Pedrito.

"That's all right," said the old man, taking a swig from his bottle. "But I didn't like the way he liked that horse."

Pedrito jumped up all excited. "What do you mean, Papa?"

"Sonny, you'd better keep an eye on Chúcaro!"

"Don't worry about that, Vaquero. I'll take care of him," warned Juan.

Pedrito rushed over to him and clutched his arm. "You won't let the mayordomo take him away from me, will you, Juan?"

"Don't you worry about that. But first let's hear the story. We might as well be prepared to face the situation. Go on, Vaquero."

"So I said, '*Buenas noches*, Señor Mayordomo,' and started to go home, but he stopped me.

"He says, 'Where did you get that pony? I hear all kinds of gossip going around.' 'What kind of gossip do you mean?' says I. 'Never mind that,' he says. 'Where

did you get him?' 'It's kind of a wild colt,' I said. 'Juan roped him for Pedrito in the outer field.' So I said, 'Buenas noches, Señor Mayordomo,' but he didn't budge. 'Now look here, Vaquero,' he says, 'the estanciero is coming.' 'Oh, the patrón,' I say. " 'That's nice, that's nice.' 'I just got a letter,' he says, 'and the patrón wants me to get a nice pony for his son Armando.' 'Well, there's plenty of ponies,' I say. 'Take your pick!' 'But he wants a gentle horse that's fast, and there is no time to break one in. You better bring that horse in tomorrow.' "

At this, Pedrito was ready to burst into tears.

"Come here to me, Pedrito." Mrs. Pizetti tried to comfort the boy, putting her arms around him. "Don't you fret. Nobody shall take Chúcaro from you."

Juan was getting impatient. "Go on with your story, Vaquero. What did you answer?"

" 'Pardon me, Señor,' I says, 'but I have nothing to do with that pony. Pedrito rides him.' 'Well, tell your son to bring him into the stable tomorrow.' 'Pardon me, Señor,' I say, 'but Pedrito has not much to say about the horse.' So the mayordomo got angry. 'You just told me it belongs to your son. Vaquero, are you drunk again?' 'No, Señor,' I say. 'If that is so, then I am right,' he says. 'You are always right, Señor,' I says. 'Then why did you say no?' 'I said, No, I am not drunk.' "

"Caramba!" cried Juan. "Get on with it!"

Carlos couldn't help laughing. "You certainly made a mess of it. But go on; it sounds crazy."

"So he says, 'If you are not drunk, then why do you talk so upside down? Now let us get this clear once and for all. I can't waste any more time. Tell me this—is Pedrito your son?' 'Si, Señor.' 'All right. Now, has he a pony?' 'He has two ponies, Señor.' 'Now don't try to confuse me, Vaquero,' he says. 'I'm talking about that wild colt he rides.' 'Yes, yes,' I says, 'he rides him, that's sure.' 'All right then,' he says, 'tell him to bring in the animal and I'll pay him for his trouble.' 'Oh,' I say, 'there is no trouble, Señor, but . . .' 'But what?' he says. 'There is no but, Señor,' I say, 'except—how could the boy bring him in if the pony is not his property?' So the Señor Mayordomo got mad, and he shook me and shouted, 'Vaquero, are *you* drunk or am *I* crazy?' So I say, 'No, Señor, *you* are all right, and I am all right. No harm

done!' Then I say, 'If you want the horse for the patrón's son, I guess you better talk to Juan about it.' 'Juan?' he cried. 'What has *he* got to do with it?' 'He sort of owns the pony, Señor,' I say. The Señor Mayordomo was really angry. He throws his sombrero right into the mud, and again he shakes me hard and shouts, '*Hombre!* Why didn't you say that before?' 'I never had a chance, Señor, I never had a chance,' I said."

"Stop! Stop it, Vaquero!" pleaded Mrs. Pizetti, choking with laughter. "I really can't stand any more. My sides ache!"

Carlos was already rolling under the table. His fat round cheeks were red like the tomato, he was laughing so hard.

"That's the best one on the mayordomo. Vaquero almost drove him crazy!"

"And the poor thing never had a chance!" added Juan, and once more the whole house roared with laughter.

The laughter that comes from the heart is terribly contagious. As Señor Pizetti came in, he scarcely had time to say *"Buenos días, amigos"* before the wild laughter swept him off his feet. He hadn't the slightest idea what it was all about, still he burst into a roar.

Pedrito was the first to come to his senses. "Now, please listen, Juan. I'm really scared. What are we going to do about it?"

"Pedrito is right," said Juan, his face once more sober. "We must talk seriously about this matter."

Señor Pizetti pulled out his pipe and filled it with coarse tobacco. "I don't know what you people are talking about," said he, and his eyes were fastened on the boy. "What is the trouble, Pedrito? Your eyes are red and full of tears. I am really at a loss. A few minutes ago you were giggling and now you are ready to weep."

"The mayordomo wants to take his pony," explained Mrs. Pizetti. "The patrón wrote him that he should have a pony ready for his son. For that little rascal Armando, you know . . ."

Señor Pizetti was about to light his pipe. "What?" he cried, holding the lighted match in his fingers. "You mean to say they want to give Chúcano to Armando? Now, I hate to be mean, but, frankly, I wouldn't even give the dust on Chúcaro's hoof to that spoiled brat. Caramba! I almost burned my fingers."

"Don't let them take him. Please, please!" begged Pedrito and pressed closer to Juan. "I would rather die."

"Don't be silly! We'll never let him have the pony." There was a gleam in Juan's eyes and weight in every word. "Chúcaro is yours, Pedrito. And they can get him only over my dead body!"

"Now, now, let us not be too hasty," Carlos warned. "After all, this is a matter of who owns what."

Mrs. Pizetti reached for the empty gourd. "Let me bring you some fresh maté. It is good for the nerves. When it comes to a question of property, you have to think it over carefully."

"What is there to think over?" cried Juan. "The pony belongs to Pedrito. And that's the end of it!"

73

Señor Pizetti put his pipe back under his belt strap. It had gone out. "Don't get excited, Juan! I am not a lawyer who knows all the questions, but I do know that the law is full of funny twists. The law may *compel* you to give up the pony. But I don't say that you should. Let me ask you this: Did you lasso Chúcaro on the patrón's property?"

"That has nothing to do with it!" said Juan angrily, pounding the table.

The old Vaquero was startled. He had dozed off again and was now blinking and trying to get the drift of the talk.

"What's up, boys? What's up?"

"Don't pay any attention to them, Vaquero," quieted Mrs. Pizetti and placed a fresh maté in his hands. "Just take a sip and go back to sleep. You've done your share."

"Let me remind you," said Carlos, directing his words to Juan. "You say that the question of property does not enter in. How do we know? Suppose it does? What happens then? All right, the patrón may not send you to prison for refusing to give up a horse. But there is one thing he can surely do . . . and do you know what I am driving at?"

"I don't see what you mean." Mrs. Pizetti was puzzled. "What *can* the patrón do to him?"

74

"Fire him!"

There was a dead silence. Everyone was stunned.

"Juan . . . fired . . ." The very idea was unbelievable.

Each one longed to go to him and say, "We are all with you, and we'll fight for you, tooth and nail." But no one uttered the words.

"*Dios mío!*" Mrs. Pizetti sighed. "What can we do?"

Then Mira appeared, the old, stray dog. Quietly he strolled around the patio, sat down for a minute, and then went sniffing from one to another until he had said "hello" to everybody.

The Vaquero placed the gourd on the table and at last broke the silence. "Come here, Mira, old fellow." And with his dry, wrinkled, shaky fingers he scratched the dog's ears. "My, my! Don't tell me your yellow hair is turning gray, too! Well, we're all getting old. But you can't complain. You've always had plenty to eat, belonged to nobody and everybody. You were always free."

"What are you mumbling about?" Carlos turned toward the old man. "I thought you were asleep."

"Who could sleep, when you all talk so loud and get so excited. I don't believe that there is much to worry about."

"You sound like an old fool. Can't you get it into your head that the question of property is a ticklish one? It

makes some people laugh and some to cry. The way you talk, it sounds as easy as when you gulp down a gallon of wine."

Sheepishly the Vaquero scratched the back of his head. "Sure, it is just as easy as you've said."

They all stared at him.

"I say, let the pony decide it *himself*."

"What do you mean?" several of them asked.

"I say," repeated the Vaquero, "let Chúcaro decide it himself."

"Caramba!" cried out Juan, striking his boots with his horsewhip. "The Vaquero is right! That's exactly what we'll do."

"But what does he mean?" insisted Mrs. Pizetti.

"What on earth could Chúcaro do about it?" cried Pedro.

"You people should understand the Vaquero by now," smiled Juan. "He talks horse sense. He doesn't speak *castellano*, he speaks the Pampa! Now I'll tell you what we'll do. We will turn Chúcaro lose and let the rascal Armando lasso him. If he can do it, well and good. The pony is his. If not, he remains with Pedrito. Don't you see? It is as clear as day."

"It certainly is," said Señor Pizetti.

"Why, it's a cinch! Armando will never be able to lasso that pony," cried Carlos, turning to Pedrito, who still looked doubtful and painfully puzzled. "Don't you worry my boy; he couldn't even lasso his own neck. But the way the shadows lie, it must be late."

They all got up.

"Well, I'm glad it's settled at last." Mrs. Pizetti heaved a sigh of relief as she shook hands with the boys. "I am only sorry that the Vaquero didn't speak up before!"

The old man took his time responding. He was fumbling with the gourd trying to squeeze another sip out of the soaking leaves. He squinted his watery eyes and grinned.

"I never had a chance, Señora, I never had a chance!"

12

AN URGENT MESSAGE

There was something about the Vaquero that many people could envy. He could fall asleep like a puppy—
anywhere. He didn't care a fig whether he was in bed or
in the saddle, standing against the barn door or lying in
the ditch—when he felt like sleeping, he slept. Once he

even fell asleep while milking a cow. He dreamt there was a cloudburst; the rain poured down in buckets until it reached his neck. Then he woke up and to his astonishment found that he was drenched in milk . . . and not a drop in the pail!

Now you can picture him snoring on the bench outside the mayordomo's office, where he had been sent by Juan with an urgent message.

"The Señor Mayordomo is busy." "The Señor Mayordomo can't see you yet," the office boy–secretary told him time and time again. It was apparent that after his baffling conversation with the old man, the mayordomo was unwilling to see him. So the Vaquero just fell asleep and snoozed off and on the whole afternoon. Then at last, just before closing time, the secretary shook him hard.

"What is it you want?"

"Oh, oh!" The Vaquero came to his senses. "Tell the Señor Mayordomo that I, the Vaquero, was here with an urgent message from Juan. It says that Chúcaro will be let loose in the big corral on Sunday after dinner. If the patrón's son, Armando, can lasso him, good for him. If not, good for Pedrito. Just tell him that."

13

THE PATRÓN

It would be unfair to paint the portrait of the average estanciero, or patrón. There is no average. The estancieros are as different as the people who work for them. Some like to take things easy and play as they go merrily along, while others dig themselves deep into their responsibilities like a steam shovel. Some are as soft as deerskin; others are so tough you can't help thinking of the quebracho. So you see, it all depends, as they say.

Our estanciero, Señor Muñez, was a very wealthy man. Sometimes his wealth was embarrassing to him. Children, and occasionally even grownups, would ask such silly questions: "If you were to count all your money, how much would it amount to?" You can well imagine how terribly uncomfortable poor Señor Muñez felt. He would absent-mindedly pluck his bushy eyebrows or rub his dry, wrinkled face with his nervous fingers. At last he would retort angrily, "How would I know? I didn't coin the darn stuff!"

Of course, he didn't. As a matter of fact, the poor man was the innocent victim of the enormous wealth showered upon him. He had inherited every penny. A few days after his father had been buried, a small army of secretaries encircled him and began firing questions at him, one after the other: "Señor Muñez, an order came in yesterday for fifty-five hundred sheepskins. Do you want us to ship from your Patagonian stock or fill only half of the order from the estancia?" Then: "Señor Muñez, your father commissioned me to change the stockrooms and the garage area of your mills at Rosario. Here are the plans for your approval." Another: "Señor Muñez, at the Santa Fe ranch the locusts destroyed about 30 per cent of the crop. You might wish to see the detailed report . . ." It went on and on.

Señor Muñez was dumbfounded. His whole life had suddenly changed. Before his father's death his whole life was play, and he felt free as the proverbial bird. Now, out of the clear sky, the things he detested most descended upon him: business affairs, commercial decisions, statistics.

The one thing he enjoyed playing with was the estancia—the family ranch. Outside of the ranch, the whole involved Muñez empire made him miserable. Day after day there were directors' meetings, business luncheons, interviews, and always, always people expecting him to make decisions, decisions, decisions! In the evening there were receptions, balls, concerts, and visiting relatives—to please the Señora.

When Señor Muñez went to bed, dead tired, he hardly had enough energy left to pick up the urgent telegram that his private secretary slipped under his bedroom door. It was from the mayordomo.

EVERYTHING ARRANGED FOR YOUR ARRIVAL SATURDAY. AM NEGOTIATING FOR WONDERFUL PONY FOR MASTER ARMANDO. DETAILS PERSONALLY.

The telegram with the good news from his favorite ranch revived him. Señor Muñez poured himself a little *aguardiente,* and then, telegram in hand, paced the enormous bedroom, thinking of the fun they'd have at the ranch. He was especially pleased about "the wonderful pony" the mayordomo mentioned for his Armando.

Now, Señor Muñez did not realize that his pet son, Armando, was a thoroughly spoiled child. Señor Muñez considered him a rather "lively" kid, but he himself was too busy to keep track of his son's affairs, which made everybody else miserable. Armando's mother, on the other hand, was completely worn out with the complaints pouring in from angry parents and teachers. At last her patience was exhausted, and she decided to let the servants and tutors struggle with Armando. She felt she could spend her time more profitably helping others, the poor and the sick and young boys and girls in orphanages and reformatories.

On Saturday morning when the patrón's party arrived, everything at the estancia appeared bright and shiny. The trees and bushes in front of the big house were neatly clipped, the road raked and swept, and every one of the sixty-five windows glistened in the sunshine.

In front of the terrace leading to the main entrance, a reception committee of four stood in a respectful row. They were the mayordomo, the chief bookkeeper, the veterinary, and—however, the fourth member cannot be counted officially, for it was Mira, the old stray dog. His only excuse for being there was that he wasn't anywhere else!

They were all dressed in their Sunday best, except the nonchalant Mira, who was chased away the moment the car pulled up.

A few steps behind this reception committee stood a young gaucho, umbrella in hand. The mayordomo had ordered him to be there to escort the Señora from the automobile to the covered patio.

The moment the car stopped, Armando ran to greet the men, and they were sprinkled with rain. But the rain did not fall from the sky. It was Armando's private little shower, which spurted out of the bouquet of flowers stuck on his lapel. A rubber ball attached to a tube made the flowers sprinkle whenever he pressed it—an old trick.

The mayordomo was the first to welcome the boy and the first to grind his teeth in anger. He had taken such pains to fix his fresh cravat and put on a stiff collar and comb his hair. And now it was all a mess. He clenched

his hands and gritted his teeth, the poor mayordomo. Still, he tried to smile.

By the time Señor Muñez and the Señora stepped out, the showy part of the impressive reception committee was soaking wet. They all had their handkerchiefs out, wiping their faces and necks.

"What's this?" asked the astonished estanciero, after he shook hands with the men. "You seem to be all wet! And not a drop of rain anywhere on the road from the station!"

"Oh, well, er . . . we . . ." mumbled the mayordomo with a forced smile. "It's just a little joke of Armando's. . . ."

"Where is that rascal? Just wait, I shall certainly do something about this!" said the patrón in anger.

But he never did anything about it. The good man had the best intentions, yet he couldn't carry them out because he was terribly absent-minded. He would say or notice something and a minute later he had forgotten about it completely.

"Well . . . well!" The patrón patted the mayordomo on the shoulder. "I am certainly happy to be here . . . so nice and quiet after the hectic rush in the city." His nervous fingers twitched and fumbled at the flower in his lapel. "Yes, yes, the city drives me crazy!"

"We are all so happy to have you here," said the mayordomo, his face wreathed in smiles.

"Yes, yes—but you can't believe half of what people say. I really don't know what the world is coming to," the patrón rambled on. "But tell me about yourself. How are the bulls, and the pigs? How is the wheat coming and how is the corn? Yes, how *is* the *maíz?*"

"Oh, everything is just fine, Señor Muñez. If the weather will just keep up like this—no hail, no locusts, God forbid—we ought to have a great harvest."

"Splendid, splendid! I am eager to know about the cattle. How many head have we now? By the way, two prize bulls are on their way. I bought the finest that were shown at the Agricultural Exposition. Twenty-five thousand pesos apiece! Well, how are things, doctor?"

It was impossible to reply to his stream of questions, as he never waited for answers, but since these words were addressed to the veterinary, he tried to speak up.

"Until a couple of weeks ago, there was no serious sickness among the cattle. . . . However . . ."

"Splendid! Splendid!"

"We were fortunate to save the herd. Out of two hundred head only forty-eight died."

"Splendid! Splendid!" the estanciero kept repeating, until at last he realized that the news was bad. "What?" he cried. "You say some of my best pure-bred cattle have died? You might as well tell me the worst! How many head have we lost in all, doctor?"

"Just as I said before, Señor, forty-eight head."

"I am terribly sorry to hear that. I've always been proud of the health of our cattle. By the way, I must tell you about the prize bulls; they are already on the way. Where is the Señora? Well, she must have gone into the house. You haven't told me about the sheep, mayordomo! I wish the bookkeeper were here. Oh, there you are! Well, well, how you have changed! You seem to have a double chin. No one has told me about the sheep."

"Oh, about the sheep, Señor, we have over seventy-five hundred. They average five pounds of wool apiece against six pounds last year."

"Splendid, splendid! But why do you talk about last year? That belongs to the past. When you feel hungry, you don't think of last night's dinner but of your next meal. Ho! Ho! Isn't that so? What I want to know is how many head have we now?"

"About seventy-five hundred, Señor."

"Splendid! But go on. What is the fleece average?"

"Five pounds per sheep, Señor."

"Well, isn't that one pound less than a year ago?"

"Si, Señor."

"Why didn't you say that in the first place? It makes all the difference in the world."

They all felt uneasy. But no one dared to speak.

"Did you say the dinner is waiting?" the patrón questioned the mayordomo. "That's splendid!"

"No, Señor."

Señor Muñez was astonished. "Well, I heard someone distinctly say *dinner*, or was it supper?"

"You mentioned it yourself, Señor," the veterinary volunteered.

"Did I mention that? How strange. We ate in the dining car hardly more than half an hour ago. . . . However, if you say it is ready, we might as well go in and eat. . . ."

The patrón seemed to be in a good humor once more. He beamed at the men, who were still furtively mopping their damp clothes. Then he looked up toward the sky and said with relief, "Thank God! It isn't raining any more," and was just about ready to enter the house when the mayordomo stepped forward.

"You will recall, Señor, that I promised in my telegram to give you details about the pony you wanted for Armando." The mayordomo winked at his colleagues, and they slowly disappeared.

"Yes, of course. But I don't see what there is to discuss, unless the pony you found is not what we want. I wrote you that he should be fast, gentle, and intelligent. Well, have you got him?"

"Yes, and no, Señor," said the mayordomo hesitantly.

"Yes and no!" the patrón cried, and his nearsighted eyes seemed sunk in a mass of wrinkles. "What do you mean?"

"Your letter came only a week ago, which left us little time. It takes time to select and break in a horse."

"With all the gauchos around?"

"They have been kept busy lately. And remember, a wild pony isn't safe unless he's been properly trained. It might break every bone in the child's body."

"Consider *me!* Armando will break every bone in *my* body! He insists on a horse of his own. And with herds of horses around, it sounds perfectly ridiculous that you couldn't find a decent pony. No, no. You can't make me believe that."

"Well, Señor, I did not say that we couldn't find the right pony. . . . On the contrary, there is a . . ."

"Now you're talking! Tell me more about it. What sort of colt is it, I mean she, or is it he?"

"He, Señor."

"Splendid!"

"Fast as the devil."

"Splendid."

"He is as tame as a lamb and very intelligent."

"How splendid."

90

"There is only a slight trouble with him. . . ."

"Hmmm. That's too bad. But couldn't the veterinary help her, or is it a he?"

"He, Señor."

"Well, if you say he can be cured, everything is splendid."

"It isn't that, Señor. He is in perfect condition, well proportioned and really beautiful."

"How splendid! But let me hear, what is the catch?"

"That someone else is riding him."

"Well, whose pony is he?"

"That's exactly the question. The pony was lassoed by Juan, one of our gauchos, way out in the open fields, and he gave it to his little friend, Pedrito."

"Juan and Pedrito? Who are they? What difference does it make *who* caught her and how, as long as she belongs to the estancia."

"You are right, Señor, but still there is a ticklish point. The gauchos have their own ideas about settling such matters. They say, 'Let the horse decide it for himself!' "

"Caramba! Since when has a pony become a judge? To make decisions? Ridiculous! Never heard a more ridiculous thing! However, you might as well go on. . . ."

"Well, you know, Señor, how gauchos are. . . . Sir, let me come to the point. They sent word to me that Chúcaro—that's the name of the pony—will be let loose. If Armando can lasso him, he may keep the pony. If not, it remains with Pedrito."

"Ho . . . ho . . . ho!" The patrón couldn't help laughing. "I really think it's a marvelous solution. Splendid! Yes, I say, let Armando show what he can do with the lasso. He ought to be pretty good at it. Took lessons all winter long from the best gaucho in the country. Cost me plenty of money! Now, tell me, when is this affair to be held?"

"Sunday after dinner in the big corral, Señor."

"I want to be there myself. I am most anxious to meet that 'horse judge,' Chúcaro. By all means we'll be there. . . . Tell me, by the way, how long ago was it that you reminded me of dinner? I find myself forgetting things. However, now I am really getting hungry. You'd better come along, mayordomo. Just watch Armando when I tell him the big news! What's the name of that horse judge again?"

"Chúcaro, Señor," said the mayordomo as they started toward the house.

"Chúcaro? How splendid! And he decides who is to be his owner! Think of that! How perfectly splendid!"

92

14

BOLAS

The ancient saying that "the eyes are the mirror of the
heart" sometimes goes out of order. For instance, looking
at Juan, you would not have guessed that this Sunday
was different from any other Sunday.

He took a generous time to dress, and when he was

through, he smeared a bit of grease on his mustache, enough to make it pliable and shiny. The twisting and twirling of his mustache was a job in itself. This business of proper training of the mustache took time, mainly because he did it in front of his favorite picture, showing the great waterfalls of the Iguazú. Every Sunday morning he made that long trip to the falls and return, which could not be done hurriedly, in spite of the fact that he traveled by the fastest known vehicle—imagination.

After breakfast, which usually consisted of coffee and a tiny loaf of white bread, he took an armful of thongs and ropes and dropped them at the side of the cart. That gauchos are not too diligent is an understatement, but working with leather and ropes intrigued Juan. And there were always such things needing attention—a broken saddle to be mended, a stirrup replaced, or a good lasso repaired.

This time he was going to make a hunting gadget typical of the Pampa. He had promised Pedrito that someday soon he would take him on an ostrich hunt. And ostrich-hunting is usually done with *bolas*, a strange but very effective weapon. It consists of three braided strips of cowhide joined together in the shape of a "Y." To each of the three ends heavy balls were attached, called the "*tres Marias*." When he throws it, the gaucho grabs the longest end of the bolas, twirling it above his head and then letting it fly. As it strikes its target, the bolas winds around the victim's legs, and the animal, of course, must fall. As with everything else, it takes practice to be able to throw the bolas accurately.

Resting his back against the high wheel of his cart, Juan started making a new bolas—a small one that would be easy for Pedrito to handle. To see a beautifully plaited lasso or bolas take shape under his skillful fingers gave him the same pride and thrill that an artist experiences when from dead canvas the living picture emerges.

Don't let Juan fool you, though. Neither his eyes nor his mind was entirely on his work. From under the rim of his sombrero, slightly tilted, he could see a lot. And a lot was going on!

Straight ahead at some distance a cloud of dust was rising near José's hut. He couldn't distinguish who they were, but there was no doubt about it, several couples were dancing—and so early in the morning! Then when the music died down a little, he could hear ponies galloping in the outer field. Every Sunday there was keen rivalry among the young gauchos as to whose pony was fastest. With terrific yelling and shouting, the race was in full swing. Juan dropped his bolas and went to the other side of the cart. The wheat field cut off part of the scene, but he could hear. He stood motionless and listened. Suddenly he heard the young boys cheering, "Chúcaro!"

He went back to his work, and his thoughts ran on. "What if Chúcaro should be roped? Suppose Armando knows how to use the lasso? What would Pedrito do? But, no! That's impossible!"

People were coming home from the church, some on horseback and some in carts, all in a great hurry to get ready for the big show.

Juan lifted his head toward the sky. "It might rain," he murmured to himself. And quickly gathering up all his leather and straps, he ran to the casita. It was too early to attend the match, but he wanted to get away. "I mustn't meet Pedrito," he thought, "until it is all over."

He changed his kerchief for the blue one, took his poncho on his arm, and went in search of his wandering gypsy, Gitana.

15

THE MATCH

Among the people on the ranch, the Vaquero was the oldest; among the cattle, Pasquala. The oldest horse was called Ososo, and the oldest dog, as you know, was Mira.

Each of them had seen a great deal in his life—the herding of thousands of cattle, the racing of numberless gaucho ponies, and the stampeding of frightened animals out on the Pampa. At the ranch itself there were weddings, lasting sometimes three days and three nights,

christening parties, great barbecues, homemade circuses
and carnivals.

But nobody had ever seen so many people as were
gathered on the day of the match around the big corral.

You know how hard the quebracho is, but this time
the strain was almost too much, even for a fence made of
this remarkable wood. So many people, climbing and
jostling, pushing, shouting and crowding. The strong

98

quebracho fence whimpered and moaned and creaked.

The heaviest crowd was gathered around the main gate, where in his shiny open car stood Señor Muñez, the estanciero himself. He was watching Armando swing his lasso in the corral.

"Well, what are you waiting for? Go to it, son, go to it!"

The crowd, hungry for some fun, burst out laughing. Even Mira pricked up his ears and began wagging his tail.

"What's the joke?" asked Señor Muñez, turning to his mayordomo. "What are they roaring about?"

The mayordomo stepped on the running board and whispered in his ear, "The corral is empty, Señor. Chúcaro isn't here yet!"

"There they come!" cried Carlos from the top of the fence. "The young rascal! He's *leading* the horse. That's why it took such an awful long time!"

Pedrito led his pony inside the gate; then he quickly disappeared. Later Juan spied him beyond the fence lying in the grass with his head buried in his arms.

For a minute the pony seemed bewildered, and he began searching the crowd. At last he noticed his friend Gitana grazing near the fence. He whinnied. In reply Gitana raised her head and neighed, and Pedrito sat up.

"How wonderful," the boy thought, "that nobody can understand their language except Juan and me." He got up and sheepishly walked over to the mare.

"Coach him, Gitana, please tell him what to do," the boy whispered. Pedro sat down on the grass. He shut his eyes, and in spite of the noisy crowd, he thought he could almost hear the ponies talking.

"Courage," murmured Pedrito. His lips moved, but no sound could be heard. Suddenly, dead silence fell upon the crowd. Pedrito opened his eyes. Armando was now ready to throw the lasso. Everyone was watching him.

There!!! The lasso sped and fell, barely touching the pony's tail.

"Splendid!" cried Señor Muñez at the top of his voice. "You almost got him, son. Let's consider this a tryout. I think he ought to have another chance!"

"Say, Juan," whispered Carlos to his friend, "the rascal handles the rope better than I thought. I wouldn't consider another chance. What do you think?"

"*Mamma mia!*" cried Mrs. Pizetti, sitting next to her friends in a gaucho chair. "And we thought he couldn't even lasso his own neck!" They all waited for a response from Juan.

"All right," Juan at last got up and shouted, addressing

100

the patrón. "Go ahead, let the boy have another chance!"

"All right, give it another try, my boy!" exclaimed Señor Muñez, waving his handkerchief at his son. But at this moment the rain began to pour down.

"What's this?" he turned to the mayordomo. "It seems you have rain here every day."

"Every day? No, Señor, there hasn't been a drop for the past three weeks."

"Now, don't tell me that! You seem to have a short memory. You were soaking wet when I met you yesterday. Let's put up the top, chauffeur. I wish this circus were over! Armado is sure to catch cold."

By the time the youngster was ready for the second round, the dusty corral was sopping wet and puddles began to appear everywhere. Armando, angered by his first fiasco, put all his strength into the second throw and slipped and fell face down in the fresh mud.

Why is it that people everywhere enjoy so much having somebody get involved with mud? It is hard to understand, yet you should have seen that crowd bursting

with laughter. The mayordomo had to use his police whistle to stop it. "Silence, everybody!" he cried, and there was fire in his eyes. "I suggest we postpone the trial and wait quietly until the shower is over. It won't last long. What do you think, Señor?"

"A splendid idea, my friend," said the estanciero, stretching his legs. "Please call Armando, and then both of you should come into the car and keep dry."

There was no need to call Armando. He came running and tore open the door. "Come in quick," the father begged. "You poor child—look at his face and hands all smeared with mud."

"Never mind!" Armando retorted and reached for a bag on the floor.

"What's that?" cried Señor Muñez "What are you going to do?"

"Just leave it to me." The boy's voice was tense with rage. "I'll fix that pony in no time. Just watch!"

He ran back to the corral and tore open the bag.

"Bolas!" cried Juan and jumped into the corral. "You can't do that! No, not that . . . !"

Gitana neighed, terrified.

"Bolas!" screamed Pedrito and ran madly after Chúcaro.

It was too late.

16

ITCHY HOOVES

Pedrito was the first to reach the pony, who lay in the mud, his body trembling. Chúcaro's eyes were half-closed and, caused by pain or rain, the tears streamed. Pedro wiped the pony's face. "Don't worry, Chúcaro."

Gitana thrust her head through the fence and whinnied.

Chúcaro scrambled to his feet, and Pedrito led him toward the gate. They couldn't get through because everybody rushed there, crowding in, to see . . .

They heard Juan cry out, as he caught Armando by the shoulders and shook him soundly. "I ought to give you a beating for that, you wretched boy! You might have killed that horse. But you won't get him! Not after this!"

"Let me go, let me go!" yelled Armando.

"Say, what's going on there?" called the mayordomo. "Let that boy alone." Juan released the lad.

The shower was now over. A cool breeze blew across the Pampa and brought the sweet scent from the cornfields.

The patrón stepped out of his car. "Just look at that boy!" he exclaimed, horrified. "He looks as if he'd been beaten!"

"No, Señor, just covered with mud."

"Papa!" cried Armando to his father. "Juan *refuses* to give me the pony!"

But Juan paid no attention to him. He went over to Chúcaro, examined him thoroughly, and quietly remarked to the other gauchos, "I don't believe any serious harm has been done. The bolas hit him under the eye. The wound will heal in no time, I'm sure."

Now Armando picked up his bolas from the ground, and when he reached the gauchos, he announced defiantly, "I don't care what you say! The pony is mine!"

"Never!" cried Juan.

"Never!" echoed Pedrito.

"Never? You'll see!" Armando laughed scornfully and threw out his chest. "You have nothing to say about it. *We* own everything here."

"You may own the whole world," retorted Pedro, "but you'll never have Chúcaro."

"My father will see about that! I just have to snap my finger and the pony is mine!"

"You'll never get my pony; you might as well quit," said Pedro.

"No?" screamed Armando. "You'll see in a minute, just wait till . . ."

Armando never finished that particular sentence! Chúcaro kicked out strongly in his direction, and Armando felt as if a bomb had exploded directly under him. The whole world was filled with bursting stars—gold, silver, and red. Armando landed with a plop in Mrs. Pizetti's lap.

Señor Muñez was enraged. "Whoever dared to call that beast a lovely gentle pony?"

The crowd, in a solid block, moved to the scene, crowding around the boy.

"Dios mío! Dios mío!"

Juan wormed his way through to Mrs. Pizetti and examined Armando.

"Get away from me, you brute!" Armando shouted, "Get away!" until at last the chauffeur picked him up and carried him to the car.

"What happened, my son, what happened? Tell me," Señor Muñez begged.

"Juan, that big good-for-nothing gaucho, let the horse kick me."

"How could that be?"

"He said, 'Kick, Chúcaro, *kick, Chúcaro, kick!*'"

"That's a lie!" cried Juan. "The pony had sense enough himself. He didn't need any coaxing."

"How dare you call my son a liar, you . . . you . . . who are you, anyway?"

"He is your gaucho, Señor. He's been on the rancho for many years."

"Well, I don't like his manners. No one shall call my son a liar. Get your pay and go! And take that beast with you. I wouldn't have that pony at any price!"

17

TO IGUAZÚ

Juan rode in front, and Pedrito followed close behind on Chúcaro. Bundles and bags hung from their saddles on either side. They had so little and still so much—clothes, a guitar, a few keepsakes, and some tools.

They might easily have been mistaken for wandering gypsies or harvest workers, moving from ranch to ranch.

There were three in the party. But the third horseman was old and carried a heavy heart. He wanted to accompany them, just for a while, till sunset. Still, he kept at a distance as if to drag out the time. He, too, had a small bundle hanging from his arm—those old things that a gaucho hands down to his son: a pair of stirrups, a silver bit, a fancy belt, and a knife. Also, Mrs. Pizetti had insisted on sending some roast chicken and bread.

It was late afternoon when they left the alfalfa fields behind and reached a narrow road cutting through the corn. There was corn everywhere. Each was enwrapped in his poncho and his thoughts. Not a word was uttered.

"Adiós!" is so easy it may be said a hundred times a day. But when the leave-taking is real and you mean the farewell, then your lips are sealed. You keep silent and go.

How can one part with friends, friends who are as close as your own arm? How can one take leave of a mud hut or a covered cart in the field? You can't shake hands with memories! What would you tell an old ombù tree and your favorite spots on a quebracho fence? Could you say adiós to ponies that you had raised and trained, and bulls and cows that you had named? And what could a boy say to an armadillo hole, to rabbits and dogs and sheep that had been his pets? No, you can't say adiós to each blade of grass.

They looked straight ahead, without a glance to the

110

left or the right. They did not turn their heads. Not once.

The sun reached the horizon. Soon the flaming sky would fade and then the dusk.

"Let's stop," Juan said, "and wait for the Vaquero to catch up." When he was near, they all dismounted.

"This bundle is for you, Pedrito," the old man said. "A mighty fine knife"—he smiled—"and some little things. . . . Oh, yes! And the chicken . . . Señora Pizetti sent it. She said something, but she was crying so hard I couldn't understand. And the boys said things, but I forget. . . ."

He plucked at his beard and stood shifting his weight from one foot to the other. Pedrito reached for a blade of grass to chew, and Juan just looked at the sky. Then the old man blinked and smiled, opened his arms and embraced them both. One kiss on the left cheek, and one on the right.

The Vaquero mounted his pony, turned toward home, and for the first time in years put his horse to the gallop.

After dusk, a breeze sprang up, and the corn stalks began to sway and there was a pleasant rustling among the leaves. It was a friendly road—straight, with no sudden turns, no beasts to frighten one, not even trees.

The sweet scent of ripe corn filled the air, and Pedrito noticed the cowboy opening his arms and breathing with

a deep sigh. Then, turning his head, a smile appeared on his face, big as the moon. The boy, too, lifted his arms and let that heavenly air flow deeper and deeper into his body. The deeper it reached, the lighter he became, and he searched under his poncho to see if his heart was still there. And so Pedrito, too, began to understand what Juan meant when he would say, "Air, pure air, can lift a heavy heart and help you to forgive and forget anything you want. If you want to!"

Pedrito stood up in the saddle and pushed back his sombrero. Every muscle in his body, every thought in his mind was now geared for adventure.

"Juan," he cried excitedly, as he rode up alongside, so close their stirrups touched. "How about the pictures on the casita wall? Did you forget them?"

"The pictures?" the gaucho repeated absent-mindedly. "Sure, I brought along a couple of them."

" 'The Good Shepherd,' I hope," said the boy quickly, "and 'The Waterfalls of the Iguazú'?"

"Yes, and the picture post card," smiled Juan and began to hum a tune. It was an old song with a tingling melody, but somehow they bumped into a funny word and they both began to laugh.

"Don't you ever worry, Pedrito; we'll have a lot of fun!"

The boy was slow responding. He wanted to say something very, very pleasing to the gaucho, but "It's wonderful that you have been fired!" was all that came from his lips. The man understood.

They rode silent for a while. Then Pedrito asked, "How long will it take us to get to the Falls?"

"God only knows. Maybe two months, maybe three. Pizetti figured from his map that we could reach it by Christmas."

"Caramba!" exclaimed the boy. "Christmas at the great falls of Iguazú! Oh, I can hardly wait!"

They had reached the end of the cornfields. Before them stretched the prairie under the stars—millions of stars, some faint and some bright, but all of them, every single one, blinking at Pedrito. Pedrito thought, "What are they trying to say?"

There was a chill in the air, and the tall grass was getting cool, ready for the dew. "This is the place to spend the night," said Juan.

"Where?" asked the boy dreamily.

"Let's camp right here where we are," the gaucho repeated. "You spread our sheepskins on the grass, woolly side up, and I'll tether the ponies!"

Sheepskins on the grass, woolly side up. The gauchos lay flat on their backs, warm and snug under their ponchos. The ponies nearby, munching the luscious grass, had no covers but the starlit sky. They felt at home, completely.

The sun was still washing his face when the gauchos were on the road again, heading north toward the falls of the Iguazú.